SMiFFY BLUE

ACE CRIME DETECTIVE

THE CASE OF THE MISSING RUBY AND OTHER STORIES

WALTER DEAN MYERS

ILLUSTRATIONS BY
DAVID J.A. SIMS

A
LITTLE
APPLE
PAPERBACK

SCHOLASTIC INC.

New York Toronto London Auckland Sydney
Mexico City New Delhi Hong Kong

No part of this publication may be reproduced in whole or in part, or stored in a retrieval system, or transmitted in any form or by any means, electronic, mechanical, photocopying, recording, or other-wise, without written permission of the publisher. For information regarding permission, write to Scholastic Inc., Attention: Permissions Department, 555 Broadway, New York, NY 10012.

ISBN 0-590-67666-0

12 11 10 9   7 8/0

Printed in the U.S.A.   23

First Scholastic trade paperback printing, December 1999

CONTENTS

SMIFFY BLUE
and the case of the stolen formula
1

SMIFFY BLUE
and the case of the missing racehorse
20

SMIFFY BLUE
and the case of the stolen yacht
39

SMIFFY BLUE
and the case of the missing ruby
57

SMIFFY BLUE

and the case
of the stolen formula

Smiffy Blue, famous crime fighter, sat in his small office. He was reading the *Doober City Gazette.* Jeremy Joe, who often helped Smiffy Blue solve crimes, sat at his own desk in the corner of the office. He was having his breakfast of donuts and milk.

"I wonder," said Jeremy Joe, leaning on his elbow, "how they put the holes in these donuts."

"It's simple, my lad," said Smiffy Blue. "They do not put the holes in the do- nuts. They wrap the donuts *around* the holes."

"Ohh," said Jeremy Joe, pleased to

have discovered the secret of making donuts.

Suddenly the telephone rang. It was Inspector Hector of the Doober City Police.

"You must come over to the Acme plant right away!" said Inspector Hector. "A top secret formula has disappeared!"

Smiffy Blue told Inspector Hector that he was on his way. He hung up the phone and put on his coat. Jeremy Joe was right behind him. So was Smiffy Blue's brave and trusty dog, Dog.

The Acme plant was on the edge of town. Doctor Von Von, the scientist, met Smiffy Blue at the front gate.

"Yesterday we announced to everyone that we had invented two new secret formulas," Doctor Von Von wailed. "One was a formula to un-pop popcorn. It is still there. The other one was a top secret formula for turning people invisible. And now it is gone!"

Smiffy Blue looked into the safe. Doctor Von Von was right. The secret for-

mula for making people disappear had disappeared.

"When did you first notice that the secret formula was missing?" Smiffy Blue asked.

"This morning when I came to work," Doctor Von Von replied. "I was about to help our janitor, Bobby Baddie, clean the floor. He needs help because he has a broken arm. Then I noticed that the safe was open."

"Are you sure that the safe was locked last night?" asked Smiffy Blue.

"Yes, I am," said the scientist. "Last night, after everyone had left, Suzette from the *Gazette* took pictures of me putting the formula into the safe and locking it!"

"I must see those pictures!" said Smiffy Blue.

Smiffy Blue and Jeremy Joe rode to the *Doober City Gazette.*

Suzette from the *Gazette* gave Smiffy Blue the pictures. In the corner of one picture, Smiffy Blue saw a small bowl. On the side of the bowl were three letters: C-A-T.

Smiffy Blue smiled. It was a slightly shy smile. And a slightly sly smile. It was the kind of smile that Smiffy Blue smiled when he had found a clue.

"Have you found a clue, Smiffy Blue?" Jeremy Joe asked.

"Indeed, I have!" said Smiffy Blue. "Do you see this bowl?"

"Yes," said Jeremy Joe.

"Do you know what these letters stand for?"

"Ooh! Ooh! I got it!" Jeremy Joe's ears twitched with excitement as he spoke. "They stand for cat. A pussycat has stolen the secret formula!"

"NO!" roared Smiffy Blue. "It stands for Criminal And Thief!"

"Oh, I didn't get it," said Jeremy Joe.

"This is the bowl from which the Criminal And Thief eats," said Smiffy

Blue. "But there is no fork or spoon about and no spots on the floor. How can the criminal eat from a bowl without a spoon and leave no spots on the floor?"

"How did he do that?" asked Jeremy Joe.

"By catching the spots in his beard!" said Smiffy Blue. "The thief is a man with a beard! We must go to the Doober City barber and ask if she knows about a man with a beard!"

Off they went to the Doober City Barber Shop. There they met Patty de Pate, the Doober City barber.

"Have you seen a man with a long beard come in here?" asked Smiffy Blue.

"Only one," said Patty de Pate. "A tall man with a long beard and squinty eyes."

"Did you say squinty eyes?" asked Smiffy Blue.

"I did," said Patty de Pate.

Smiffy Blue smiled. It was a shy smile. It was a sly smile. It was the kind of smile that Smiffy smiled when he had found a clue.

"That means the thief has misplaced his glasses! That is why he squints! The thief is a man with squinty eyes and a beard! He will probably go to the glasses store to buy a new pair of glasses. We must go there also!"

"You have to find him quickly!" said Doctor Von Von, who had arrived with Inspector Hector in the Doober City police car. "For if he sells the secret formula to our enemies in Enemyville, we will be lost!"

"Never fear," said Smiffy Blue. "We will find him soon enough. Now, on to the glasses store!"

And off they went. Smiffy Blue's scarf flew behind him as Jeremy Joe pedaled the bicycle until he was quite red in the face.

At the glasses store Smiffy Blue looked around carefully, letting nothing escape his keen eye.

"Do you need glasses?" asked Doctor Seymour Orless, the man who ran the glasses store.

"Hardly," replied the famous detective. "I am Smiffy Blue, the famous detective, and this is Jeremy Joe, who often helps me solve crimes. Have you seen anyone with a long beard and squinty eyes who looks as if he might have stolen a secret formula?"

"No," said Doctor Seymour Orless. "The only one who came in here today was a man wearing a nice blue suit and a blue silk tie."

Smiffy Blue covered his mouth with his fingers. But Jeremy Joe could tell that he was smiling. It was a shy kind of smile. It was a sly kind of smile. It was the kind of smile that Smiffy Blue smiled when he had found a clue.

"Smiffy Blue has found another clue!" cried Jeremy Joe.

"I have indeed found a clue!" said Smiffy Blue. "Indeed, I have!"

"What is that clue?" Jeremy Joe asked.

"Why," asked Smiffy Blue, "would the thief wear a blue silk tie?"

"Ooh! Ooh! I've got it!" said Jeremy Joe. "He wears it 'cause he likes that tie?"

"NO!" roared Smiffy Blue. "He wears it to cover up his beard! But . . ."

"Here comes the but," said Jeremy Joe.

". . . we know that he must have a very long beard to catch any drops of gravy that fall as he eats," said Smiffy Blue.

"True, true, Smiffy Blue!" said Jeremy Joe.

"Then he must have bought a very big tie," said Smiffy Blue, "which means he is a rich man! Therefore we must go to the Doober City Rich Man's Club at once!"

"That we must do, Smiffy Blue!" said Jeremy Joe.

The Doober City Rich Man's Club was the tallest building in Doober City. There they met Stash McCash, the richest man in Doober City.

"Is there a tall, squinty-eyed rich man in the Rich Man's Club who is wearing a blue silk tie and who looks as if he might have just stolen a secret formula?" asked Smiffy Blue.

"No, there is not," said Stash McCash. "But just this morning I saw a tall, squinty-eyed rich man headed toward the Doober City Post Office. He had a letter in his hand."

"A letter did you say?" asked Smiffy Blue. "Then we must act quickly. Come, we must hurry to the Doober City Post Office!"

So Smiffy Blue and Jeremy Joe and Dog hurried to the Doober City Post Office. They got there just before Penny

Stampp, the mail clerk, was leaving.

"Quick!" said Smiffy Blue. "Tell me if you have seen a tall, bearded man with squinty eyes, wearing a blue silk tie today."

"No," said Penny Stampp, "we had only one customer today. A man wearing a trench coat bought an envelope. He also had a determined look on his face!"

"And did he also buy a stamp?" asked Smiffy Blue.

"No," said Penny Stampp.

"And the determined look — " said Smiffy Blue. "Are you sure about that?"

"I am sure," Penny said.

Then Smiffy Blue smiled. It was a shy smile. And a sly smile. It was the kind of smile that Smiffy Blue smiled when he had found a clue.

"Smiffy Blue has found *another* clue!" said Jeremy Joe.

"Yes," said Smiffy Blue. "Indeed, I have. I know where the thief is going next! Quick! Call Inspector Hector and tell him to meet me at the Acme plant. Also, call Suzette from the *Gazette* so she can come and take a picture of the thief."

Jeremy Joe called Inspector Hector and the *Gazette*'s Suzette. Then he and Smiffy Blue got on their bicycle, with Dog on the crossbar, and rode as fast as Jeremy Joe's legs could pedal to the Acme plant. When they got there they found Inspector Hector, Suzette, and Doctor Von Von waiting for them. As they gathered around the safe, Bobby Baddie, the janitor, swept the floor.

"Why do you think the thief will come back here?" asked Jeremy Joe.

"What did the thief steal?" asked Smiffy Blue.

"Why, everyone knows he stole the secret formula!" replied Doctor Von Von.

"But he made a mistake," said Smiffy Blue. "It was the other formula that he wanted, not the one that made people disappear. And the determined look on his face meant that he was determined to come back and get the right formula this time."

"But the only one here is Bobby Baddie," said Doctor Von Von.

"Exactly," said Smiffy Blue. "Arrest him at once!"

"Curses!" said Bobby Baddie as Inspector Hector grabbed him, and Suzette from the *Gazette* snapped his picture. "How did you know it was me?"

"Yes, how did you know that?" asked Jeremy Joe.

"Simple, my lad," said Smiffy Blue. "I noticed a ticket to Enemyville sticking out of Bobby Baddie's pocket. He has a friend in another city but did not go there. In other words, he un-visited his friend. He also had a letter but he did not buy a stamp! So he un-mailed the letter. Now he has returned to get the secret formula that un-pops popcorn!"

"Oh, you are such a great detective," said Jeremy Joe.

"One day you, too, will be a great detective," said Smiffy Blue. "But it takes time, my son. It takes time."

"True, true, Smiffy Blue," Jeremy Joe said. "True, true."

SMIFFY BLUE

and the case
of the missing racehorse

Smiffy Blue, famous crime fighter, was reading the *Doober City Gazette.* Jeremy Joe, who often helped Smiffy Blue solve crimes, sat at his own desk.

"I wonder," said Jeremy Joe, holding his hands before him, "what makes a person right-handed or left-handed."

"It's simple, my lad," said Smiffy Blue. "Pencils make you right-handed or left-handed."

"How do they do that?" asked Jeremy Joe.

"If you always hold your pencil in your right hand when you write, you will be right-handed. If you always hold the pencil in your left hand when you write, you will be left-handed."

"Ooh," said Jeremy Joe, pleased to know the secret of being right- or left-handed.

Suddenly the telephone rang. It was

Inspector Hector of the Doober City Police.

"We need your help at once!" said Inspector Hector. "Doober City's fastest racehorse, Omar Gosh, has disappeared!"

"I'll be right over," said Smiffy Blue.

Smiffy hung up the phone and put on

his hat and scarf. Jeremy Joe was right behind him. So was Smiffy Blue's brave and trusty dog, Dog.

The Upson Downs Racetrack was two miles outside of Doober City. Inspector Hector was already there when Smiffy Blue and Jeremy Joe arrived. Petey Punter, who owned the racetrack, was

with Inspector Hector. So was Sammy Slick, the stable boy.

"Last night Omar Gosh was standing right here in his blue-and-gold blanket," said Petey Punter. "But this morning when I came into the stall to check on him, he was gone! I am so upset!"

"I had just taken my new pet camel for a walk," said Sammy Slick. "When I returned, Omar Gosh was gone."

"What evil person would steal a race-horse?" asked Inspector Hector.

"An evil person who will soon be in jail!" replied Smiffy Blue.

"But there are no clues," said Petey Punter. "When I came to the stall, the gate was open. The stall was empty except for this half-eaten apple."

Smiffy Blue looked at the gate very carefully. He frowned. Then he looked at the apple very carefully. Then he smiled. It was a shy smile. It was a sly smile. It was the kind of smile that Smiffy Blue smiled when he had found a clue.

"Smiffy Blue has found a clue!" Jeremy Joe said.

"And indeed, I have," said Smiffy Blue. "This apple has teeth marks on it! Big, thick, teeth marks! Do you know what that means?"

"The horse was eating the apple?" asked Jeremy Joe.

"NO!" roared Smiffy Blue. "It was the thief who left this clue. We must look for a thief with big, thick teeth!"

"Where are we going to look for a thief with big, thick teeth, Smiffy Blue?" asked Jeremy Joe.

"At the Doober City Dentist," said Smiffy Blue.

Micky Molar, the dentist, had just finished with a patient when Smiffy Blue arrived.

"Have you seen anyone with big, thick teeth who looks as if he had just stolen a famous racehorse?" asked Smiffy Blue.

"Well, not anyone with really big teeth," Micky Molar responded. "But yesterday a tall man with a swollen jaw and a bad toothache came in."

"What did he have to say?" asked Smiffy Blue.

"Well," said Micky Molar, "I could hardly understand him. He was holding his jaw and making odd sounds."

"Odd sounds?" asked Smiffy Blue. "What kind of odd sounds?"

"Sounded like 'Ow!' and 'Oochy Ouchy!'" said Micky Molar.

"Ow?" repeated Smiffy Blue. "Oochy Ouchy?"

Smiffy Blue's top lip curled into a smile. It was a shy kind of smile. It was a sly kind of smile. It was the kind of smile that Smiffy Blue smiled when he had found a clue.

"Smiffy Blue has found another clue!" Jeremy Joe said.

"The thief must be someone from another country!" said Smiffy Blue. "That is why the dentist could not understand him!"

"True, true, Smiffy Blue," Jeremy Joe said, wondering why he had not thought of that wonderful clue. "True, true."

"Yesterday a large ocean liner came to the dock," said Smiffy Blue. "We must go there at once and see if it brought any people from another country to Doober City."

Off they went to the dock.

At the dock they found a large ocean liner, the *Doober City Clipper.* Captain Ovida Waves was standing on its deck.

"We are looking for a thief," said

Smiffy Blue. "Did you bring anyone from another country who has big, thick teeth and who looked as if he might steal a famous racehorse?"

"Well, let me see," said Captain Ovida Waves. "Yesterday I brought six strangers to Doober City. They were all seasick. Three left the dock by taxi. Two went away in the Doober City bus. The sixth man just walked away. He was whistling."

Smiffy Blue turned around as quickly as he could. But it was not quick enough. For Jeremy Joe had already seen the smile that was spreading across his face. It was a small, shy smile. It was a small, sly smile. It was the kind of smile that Smiffy Blue smiled when he had found a clue.

"Smiffy Blue has found another clue!"

Jeremy Joe's ears wiggled with the excitement of it all.

"I most certainly have!" said Smiffy Blue. "Only one of the strangers walked away — why did he walk?"

"Ooh! Ooh! I have it! I have it!" cried Jeremy Joe. "He walked away because he likes to walk."

"NO!" roared Smiffy Blue. "Because he had nothing to ride on! Which is why he stole Omar Gosh, the fastest racehorse in Doober City!"

"Ooh, that is such a good clue!" Jeremy Joe said, putting his head on Smiffy Blue's shoulder. "That is a wonderful clue."

"It is not hard to find such clues, my lad," said Smiffy Blue, adjusting his scarf, "when you are a famous crime fighter."

"But where did that stranger go?" asked Jeremy Joe.

"He was whistling when he left the dock," said Smiffy Blue. "Therefore, he must be a musician. We must go to the Doober City Band and see if they have hired anyone new."

"That we must do, Smiffy Blue," Jeremy Joe said. "That we must do!"

The trip to find the Doober City Band was harder than Smiffy Blue and Jeremy Joe and Dog thought it would be. The band was marching in a parade, and Jeremy Joe had to pedal very hard up a very steep hill. The crime fighters caught up to the band just as the parade ended at the Doober City Town Hall.

"We are looking for a thick-toothed, seasick thief who whistles," Jeremy Joe

said to Timmy Tempo, leader of the band. "Have you seen him?"

"No, I have not," answered Timmy Tempo. "But I did see a stranger standing on the corner, watching the parade. He was wearing purple plaid pants, with his hands in his pockets."

"With his hands in his what?" asked Smiffy Blue.

"In his pockets," repeated Timmy Tempo.

Smiffy Blue smiled a big smile. It was a shy smile. And a sly smile. It was the kind of smile that Smiffy Blue smiled when he had found a clue.

"Smiffy Blue has found another clue!" said Jeremy Joe.

"Indeed, I have," said Smiffy Blue.

"Ooh! Ooh! I've got it!" said Jeremy Joe. "We have to find somebody with purple plaid on their pockets!"

"No, no, my lad," said Smiffy Blue. "There are many people with pairs of plaid pants pockets, and even many with pairs of purple plaid pants pockets. That is not the clue. The clue is where he had his hands."

"I haven't got it again!" said Jeremy Joe sadly.

"We must go back to the Upson Downs Racetrack at once!" Smiffy Blue said. "But first we must call Inspector Hector and Suzette from the *Gazette*. Tell Inspector Hector to bring handcuffs to arrest the thief!"

So Smiffy Blue and Jeremy Joe and Dog rode out to the Upson Downs Racetrack. They waited until Inspector Hector and Suzette from the *Gazette* arrived, and then they went to Omar Gosh's stall.

Smiffy Blue looked around the stall once more. He looked very carefully, letting nothing escape his trained eye.

"When you arrived this morning," Smiffy Blue asked Petey Punter, "what color sweater were you wearing?"

"A green one, with thin, red stripes," said Petey Punter.

"And you, Sammy Slick?" asked Smiffy Blue. "What kind of sweater were you wearing?"

"Why, none at all," said Sammy Slick.

Smiffy Blue smiled. It was kind of a shy smile. It was kind of a sly smile. It was the kind of smile that Smiffy Blue smiled when he had found a clue.

"Smiffy Blue has found another clue!" said Jeremy Joe.

"Better than that, I have found the thief!" said Smiffy Blue. "Why did Petey

Punter wear a green sweater with thin, red stripes this morning?"

"Because he liked that sweater?" asked Jeremy Joe.

"No!" said Smiffy Blue. "Because it was a cool morning! Which is why the man in the purple plaid pants had his hands in his pockets! And why did Sammy Slick not wear a green sweater with thin, red stripes?"

"Because he doesn't like green sweaters with thin, red stripes?" asked Jeremy Joe in a weak voice.

"NO!" roared Smiffy Blue. "Because he is the thief!"

Sammy Slick was so surprised Smiffy Blue had found him out that he jumped back and accidentally knocked the humps off his camel, which was not a camel at all, but Omar Gosh, Doober City's fastest racehorse. Quick as a wink, Inspector Hector pounced on Sammy Slick and put him in handcuffs.

"Ugh!" said Sammy Slick. "How did you know it was me?"

"Yes," said Jeremy Joe. "How did you know that?"

"The thief needed either a sweater or a blanket to keep warm," said Smiffy Blue. "That is why Petey Punter wore a sweater. But Sammy Slick did not have a sweater. It was not Omar Gosh that Sammy Slick wanted to steal. He wanted to steal the blanket, and Doober City's fastest racehorse just happened to be under it!"

"That was a truly wonderful clue, Smiffy Blue," Jeremy Joe said as Suzette from the *Gazette* took their picture. "But I didn't see it again. Maybe I'm never going to see those wonderful clues."

"One day you will," said Smiffy Blue. "It takes time to become a great detective."

"True, true, Smiffy Blue," Jeremy Joe said, pedaling back to their office. "True, true."

OMAR GOSH

SMIFFY BLUE

and the case
of the stolen yacht

Smiffy Blue, famous crime fighter, sat in his small office. He was reading the *Doober City Gazette*. Jeremy Joe, who often helped Smiffy Blue solve crimes, sat at his own desk. He was having a game of checkers with himself.

"I never win a game of checkers when I play myself!" said Jeremy Joe. "I have just lost five games in a row!"

"Indeed!" said Smiffy Blue. "Have you ever considered the idea that you just might be cheating?"

"No," said Jeremy Joe. "I have not."

So Smiffy Blue jumped up from his chair and went to the closet. He opened the closet and took out a large mirror, which he placed a few feet from Jeremy Joe.

"There," said Smiffy Blue. "Now if you cheat yourself you will surely notice it."

"That is a good idea," said Jeremy Joe. As he played he kept a sharp eye on himself to make sure that he did not cheat.

Suddenly the telephone rang. It was Inspector Hector from the Doober City Police.

"Are you quite sure?" Smiffy Blue asked calmly into the telephone.

"Yes, I am!" said Inspector Hector. "The Mayor's new yacht has been stolen!"

"Where was the boat when it was taken?" asked Smiffy Blue.

"It was down at the waterfront," said Inspector Hector.

Smiffy Blue put on his coat and hat and started for the waterfront. Jeremy Joe was right behind him. Behind Jeremy Joe came Smiffy Blue's faithful dog, Dog.

"Do you think that Dog can sniff out clues at the waterfront?" Jeremy Joe asked.

"That's *my* job," replied Smiffy Blue.

Inspector Hector met them at the waterfront. So did Matt Tropolis, the Mayor of Doober City. Nick Nasty, who just that day had opened Doober City's first floating restaurant, was there, too. Inspector Hector showed them the spot where the Mayor's yacht had been anchored.

"You must find my boat!" said Matt Tropolis. "I have promised to take the children of Doober City for a boat ride this weekend."

Smiffy Blue looked around the waterfront carefully, letting nothing escape his trained eye.

"Did you see any suspicious people around this morning?" Smiffy Blue asked the Mayor.

"No, I did not," said the Mayor. "Only

a small man feeding bread crumbs to the pigeons."

Smiffy Blue smiled. It was a slightly shy smile. And a slightly sly smile. It was the kind of smile that Smiffy Blue smiled when he had found a clue.

"Have you found a clue, Smiffy Blue?" Jeremy Joe asked.

"Indeed, I have!" replied Smiffy Blue. "Why was a man feeding bread crumbs to the pigeons?"

"Because the pigeons were hungry?" asked Jeremy Joe.

"NO!" roared Smiffy Blue. "The thief was eating bread when he stole the Mayor's yacht. He was feeding his left-over crumbs to the pigeons to get rid of the evidence! We must go to the bakery at once!"

Off they went as fast as they could to the Doober City Bakery.

Smiffy Blue looked behind the jelly donuts, and under a peach cobbler. Jeremy Joe looked at the birthday cakes, and Dog sniffed everything.

"May I help you?" asked Cheri Pye, the baker.

"Have you seen a man who likes to eat bread and who looks as if he might have stolen the Mayor's new yacht?" asked Smiffy Blue.

"No, I have not," said Cheri Pye. "But I did see two women dressed in black who bought a dozen hot cross buns."

"Did you say a dozen hot cross buns?" Smiffy Blue asked.

"Yes, I did," replied Cheri Pye.

Jeremy Joe looked at the hot cross

buns that were left in the case. Then he looked at Smiffy Blue.

Smiffy Blue was smiling. It was a shy smile. It was also a sly smile. It was the kind of smile Smiffy Blue smiled when he had found a clue.

"Smiffy Blue has found another clue!" said Jeremy Joe.

"Indeed, I have," said Smiffy Blue. "Why do you think those women in black bought a dozen hot cross buns?"

"To eat them for lunch?" asked Jeremy Joe.

"No, no, my boy," Smiffy Blue said. He had already put on his scarf. "To feed a group of people. And what does it take to carry away a boat?"

"A strong thief?" Jeremy Joe asked.

"No, no," said Smiffy Blue. "It takes a group of people. We must go to a place where there is a group of people who dress in black."

"Where would that be?" asked Jeremy Joe.

"The convent!" said Smiffy Blue.

The convent was all the way on the other side of Doober City. It took Smiffy Blue and Jeremy Joe and Dog almost an hour to reach it.

They knocked on the convent door and Sister Wisteria, the Mother Superior, answered.

"Yes, may I help you?" she said, sweetly.

"I am Smiffy Blue, the famous detective. May I come in?" asked Smiffy Blue as he came in.

"Yes, you may," said Sister Wisteria.

"Have you seen a group of people wearing dark clothing who look as if

they might have just stolen the Mayor's new yacht?"

"I have not," said Sister Wisteria.

"Hmmmm," said Smiffy Blue.

"Hmmmm," repeated Jeremy Joe, looking very wise.

"And do you keep hot cross buns in your pantry?" asked Smiffy Blue.

"No, there are no hot cross buns in our pantry that I know of," said Sister Wisteria.

Sister Wisteria led them to the pantry. She had a large key on a chain about her waist, and she used it to open the pantry door.

Smiffy Blue took out his flashlight and

looked inside the pantry. Nothing escaped his trained eye.

"Aha!" he said. "There are no hot cross buns here!"

"I did not think so," said Sister Wisteria. "But this morning we did give a sandwich to a man with a backpack. He said he was so hungry he could eat a worm."

"Did you say a worm?" Smiffy Blue asked.

"I did," replied Sister Wisteria, the Mother Superior.

Smiffy Blue smiled. It was a shy smile, almost a sly smile. It was the kind of smile that Smiffy Blue smiled when he had found a clue.

"Smiffy Blue has found another clue!" said Jeremy Joe.

"And so I have!" said Smiffy Blue. "Why did the man say he could eat a worm?"

"Because he was very hungry?" Jeremy Joe asked.

"No," said Smiffy Blue. "He did not want to eat the worm at all. He wanted to catch a fish with the worm! The thief likes to eat fish!"

"Oh, that's the best clue yet!" said Jeremy Joe.

"There is no time for congratulations," Smiffy Blue said. "We must rush to the floating restaurant at once to see if anyone has come in who wants to eat fish and looks as if he might have just stolen the Mayor's yacht. Call Inspector Hector and tell him to meet us."

When Inspector Hector arrived at the

dock they all got into a small boat and went out to the new floating restaurant in the harbor.

Smiffy Blue, Jeremy Joe, Dog, and Inspector Hector sat at the long counter.

"Would you like to see a menu?" asked Nick Nasty, the owner of the restaurant.

"Did anyone come to the restaurant

in the morning and ask for a fish to eat?" asked Smiffy Blue. "Someone who looked as if he might have just stolen the Mayor's yacht?"

"Why, I don't know," said Nick Nasty. "I was sick on the way to the dock, so I stopped off to see Doc Terdoom. When I reached the dock the Mayor's yacht had already been stolen."

"Sick? Did you say sick?" Smiffy asked. "And on your way to work?"

"That I did," said Nick Nasty. "I was sick until I got to work at my new restaurant."

Smiffy Blue smiled. It was kind of a sly smile. And kind of a shy smile. It was the kind of smile that Smiffy Blue smiled when he had found a clue.

"Smiffy Blue has found another clue!"

Jeremy Joe said. He jumped into the air and clicked his heels.

"No," Smiffy Blue said. "I have solved the crime!"

"Who is the criminal?" asked Inspector Hector.

"Yes," repeated Jeremy Joe, "who is the criminal?"

"Inspector Hector, arrest Nick Nasty! He has stolen the Mayor's yacht!"

"Oh! Oh, phooey!" said Nick Nasty.

Nick Nasty tried to run. He ran through the door that said KITCHEN.

Only there was no kitchen. There was just a yacht. On the side of it was a sign that read MAYOR'S YACHT.

Inspector Hector grabbed Nick Nasty quickly and put the handcuffs on him.

"How did you know that he was the one who did it?" Jeremy Joe asked as he rowed Smiffy Blue and Dog back to shore.

"Simple, my lad," Smiffy Blue said. "What happened to Nick Nasty on the way to the restaurant?"

"He said he was sick," Jeremy Joe said.

"Exactly," said Smiffy Blue. "Some people get seasick, but Nick Nasty gets land sick. He stole the Mayor's yacht so he could be at sea and not get land sick."

"That was a good clue," said Jeremy Joe, "but I didn't get it again."

"One day you will," said Smiffy Blue. "It takes time to be a great detective."

"True, true, Smiffy Blue," Jeremy Joe said. "True, true."

SMIFFY BLUE
and the case
of the missing ruby

Smiffy Blue, famous crime fighter, sat in his small office. He was reading the *Doober City Gazette*. Jeremy Joe, who often helped Smiffy Blue solve crimes, twirled his new umbrella.

"I wonder what keeps the raindrops up in the sky?" said Jeremy Joe. "Why doesn't it rain all the time?"

"That is simple, my lad," said Smiffy Blue, looking up from his paper. "It is

the heat of the sun that keeps up the rain."

"How does it do that, Smiffy Blue?" asked Jeremy Joe.

"When it is cool, the rain falls from

the clouds, and we get wet. But when the sun is very hot, it dries the rain before it reaches us. That is why it only rains on days when it is not sunny and warm."

"Ooh," said Jeremy Joe, pleased to know why it didn't rain all the time.

Suddenly the telephone rang. It was Inspector Hector of the Doober City Police.

"Come over to the museum right away!" said Inspector Hector. "The famous ruby of Mora Mora has been stolen!"

Smiffy Blue told Inspector Hector that he would leave right away. He and Jeremy Joe got on their bicycle. Dog, Smiffy Blue's faithful dog, went with them.

When they arrived at the museum, the

first one to greet them was Professor Lessor. He looked very upset.

"Girard the Guard was outside the door," he said, "but he did not see the thief."

Suzette from the *Gazette* was taking pictures.

"Oh, me! Oh, my, my!" Professor Lessor wrung his hands. "The ruby was in the crown of the king of Mora Mora. He lent it to us so that we could let the people of

Doober City see it. Now the king will be furious!"

Smiffy Blue looked at the case. The crown was sitting on a velvet pillow. But where the ruby was supposed to be, there was just a big hole.

"When did you last see the ruby?" asked Smiffy Blue.

"I checked it before I left last night, and then I locked the door," said Professor Lessor. "Suzette from the *Gazette* took a picture as I checked it."

Suzette showed Smiffy Blue the picture.

"Were there any clues?" Smiffy Blue asked.

"Only this empty notebook," said Inspector Hector.

"Let me see it at once!" said Smiffy Blue.

Smiffy Blue looked at the book carefully. All of the pages were indeed empty. Smiffy Blue smiled. It was a shy smile. It was a sly smile. It was the kind of smile that Smiffy Blue smiled when he had found a clue.

"Smiffy Blue has found a clue!" cried Jeremy Joe.

"Yes, I have!" said Smiffy Blue. "This is an address book!"

"But there are no addresses in the book," said Inspector Hector.

"Exactly," said Smiffy Blue. "Which means the thief doesn't know anyone around here! Therefore, he must be a stranger!"

"That's a good clue!" said Jeremy Joe.

"We must go to the Doober City Hotel," Smiffy Blue said. "I have noticed quite a few strangers staying there lately."

So Smiffy Blue and Jeremy Joe and Dog jumped upon their bicycle and hurried over to the Doober City Hotel. There they talked to Chubby Checkin, the hotel clerk.

"Do you have a stranger staying here today who looks as if he has just stolen a famous ruby?" asked Smiffy Blue.

"No," said Chubby Checkin. "We have had very few strangers here lately. And the only one we did have left early this morning."

"We must search the room in which he stayed," said Smiffy Blue.

So Chubby Checkin took Smiffy Blue and Jeremy Joe to the stranger's room. They looked all around. They looked under the rug and under the lamp. They looked in the closet and under the bed.

"There is nothing in the closet," said

Jeremy Joe, "except this old newspaper."

"Let me see it," said Smiffy Blue.

Smiffy Blue looked at the old newspaper. He rubbed it with his finger. He smelled it. He held it up to the light. Then he smiled. It was a shy smile. It was a sly smile. It was the kind of smile that Smiffy Blue smiled when he had found a clue.

"Ooh! Ooh!" said Jeremy Joe, "Smiffy Blue has found another clue!"

"Indeed, I have," said Smiffy Blue. "This is an old newspaper!"

"I've got it!" said Jeremy Joe. "The thief likes to read old newspapers."

"NO!" roared Smiffy Blue. "You use old newspapers to wrap up fish! The thief must have been to the fish market!"

"I haven't got it," said Jeremy Joe.

They went quickly to the Doober City Fish Market. Peter Porgy, the fish man, asked Smiffy Blue what they wanted.

"Did a stranger, a stranger who looked as if he might steal a precious ruby, come here to buy a fish?" asked Smiffy Blue.

"No," said Peter Porgy, "but yesterday a stranger did come here. He bought a lobster."

"A lobster?" said Smiffy Blue.

"Yes," said Peter Porgy, "and under his left arm was a can of gold paint."

Smiffy Blue rubbed his chin. Then he

paced up. Then he paced down. Then he scratched his ear. Then, slowly, slowly, Smiffy Blue began to smile. It was a shy smile. It was a sly smile. It was the kind of smile that Smiffy Blue smiled when he had found a clue.

"You have a clue, Smiffy Blue?" Jeremy Joe asked.

"Indeed, I have!" said Smiffy Blue. "The thief bought a lobster and he had gold paint. What he must have done was to paint the lobster gold. Then he must have trained the lobster to sneak into the museum and steal the crown. If someone saw the lobster in the case he would think it was part of the crown!"

"That has to be one very smart thief," said Jeremy Joe.

"Never fear," said Smiffy Blue. "We will soon track him down. Let us go quickly to the paint store and find out who bought a can of gold paint."

When they arrived at the paint store Jeremy Joe was huffing and puffing.

"Did you sell a jar of gold paint to a stranger yesterday?" Smiffy Blue asked. "A stranger who looked like he might steal a ruby from the king of Mora Mora's crown?"

"Yesterday?" Art Decoe, the paint man, scratched his head. "Yesterday, I sold two jars of gold paint. One to a schoolteacher and one to a little man carrying a poodle. I also sold him a jar of red paint but no brush."

"Did you say no brush?" asked Smiffy Blue.

"I did," said Art Decoe, the paint man.

"And did you say he was carrying a poodle?"

"He said that, too, Smiffy Blue," Jeremy Joe said.

Smiffy Blue brought his lips tightly together. Then he looked up at the ceiling. Then he shut his eyes as tightly as he could. But it was no use. Jeremy Joe saw that he was beginning to smile. At first it was just a very shy smile. Then it became a slightly sly smile. Then it became the smile that Smiffy Blue smiled when he had found a clue.

"Smiffy Blue has found another clue!" cried Jeremy Joe. "He has found the best clue yet!"

"And indeed, I have, my lad," said Smiffy Blue. "First the thief came into the museum. Then he opened the back door and let in the poodle."

"The poodle stole the ruby!" said Jeremy Joe.

"NO!" roared Smiffy Blue. "The poodle carried the lobster to the crown. Then the lobster grabbed the ruby, jumped back onto the poodle, and the poodle returned to his evil master."

"Ooh, Smiffy Blue," Jeremy Joe sighed, "that's such a good clue, I think I'm going to cry!"

"But now we must get back to the mu-

seum at once," said Smiffy Blue. "Call Inspector Hector and Suzette from the *Gazette.* Tell Inspector Hector to bring his handcuffs and be ready to arrest the thief!"

By the time Smiffy Blue and Jeremy Joe and Dog got back to the Doober City Museum it had started to rain. Jeremy Joe put up his new umbrella and held it over Smiffy Blue.

Inspector Hector, Professor Lessor, and Suzette were waiting at the museum for Smiffy Blue.

"Have you found out who stole the ruby?" asked Professor Lessor.

"No," said Smiffy Blue. "But I know how it was stolen."

"The lobster did it, and the poodle did it, and a stranger, too," said Jeremy Joe proudly.

"I don't know what you are talking about," said Professor Lessor.

"Let me look about the room once more," said Smiffy Blue.

Smiffy Blue looked all over the room. He looked in the corners and on the floor. He looked at the ceiling and the walls. He scratched his head. He rubbed his chin. Then he looked as if he were about to grin. But it wasn't exactly a grin. It was more of a smile. It was more of a shy smile, and a sly smile. It was more the kind of smile that Smiffy Blue smiled when he had found a clue.

"Ohh! Ohh!" Jeremy Joe's ears twitched with delight. "Smiffy Blue has found another clue!"

"Better than that, my lad," said Smiffy Blue. "I have found the thief!"

"How did you do that?" asked Jeremy Joe.

"The poodle carried the lobster into the museum," said Smiffy Blue. "The lobster, cleverly disguised as the royal crown of the king of Mora Mora, grabbed the ruby, then hopped upon the back of the poodle and took it to his master."

"But how will we find his master?" asked Inspector Hector.

"Very simply," said Smiffy Blue. "The paint man said that he did not sell a paintbrush to the thief. Then how did the thief paint the lobster?"

"How did he do it, Smiffy?" asked Suzette from the *Gazette*.

"With his mustache!" roared Smiffy Blue, pointing toward Girard the Guard, who had a mustache.

"Oh, no," said Girard the Guard. "The famous detective has found me out! I must get away!"

But it was already too late. Inspector Hector had put the handcuffs on him, and Suzette from the *Gazette* had taken his picture just as the ruby fell from his jacket.

"You must now go to jail!" said Inspector Hector as he led Girard the Guard away.

"But I have no lobster, and I have no poodle," Girard the Guard called out.

"Mere details, my boy," said Smiffy Blue. "Mere details."

"That mustache was a wonderful clue," said Jeremy Joe as they were leaving. "But I didn't get it."

"One day you will," said Smiffy Blue.

"It takes time to become a great detective."

"True, true, Smiffy Blue," Jeremy Joe said as he pedaled home. "True, true."

Walter Dean Myers is the acclaimed author of numerous books, including two Newbery Honor Books, *Somewhere in the Darkness* and *Scorpions*, and four Coretta Scott King Award winners. He received the 1994 *SLJ*/YALSA Margaret A. Edwards Award for Outstanding Literature for Young Adults — the most prestigious award in its field. His novel *The Glory Field* is an ALA Best Book for Young Adults, and his picture book, *Harlem*, illustrated by his son, Christopher Myers, received a 1998 Caldecott Honor Award. The inspiration for the Smiffy Blue stories comes from a game the author played with his son, in which he made each story sillier than the next and challenged his son to guess the ending. Mr. Myers lives in Jersey City, New Jersey, with his family.

David J. A. Sims began his art career at an early age when he sold his paintings to his fellow fifth graders. Today he continues his career in illustration and business. Mr. Sims is the co-founder of Big City Comics, Inc., publisher of *Brotherman: Dictator of Discipline,* an African-American best-selling comic book. *Brotherman* has been featured nationally on CNN. Mr. Sims lives in Philadelphia with his wife and son.

Also by
Walter Dean Myers

❑ BDU0-590-29912-3   *Malcolm X: By Any Means Necessary* $5.99

❑ BDU0-590-40943-3   *Fallen Angels* $4.99

❑ BDU0-590-42412-2   *Somewhere in the Darkness* $4.50

❑ BDU0-590-45896-5   *Shadow of the Red Moon* $4.50

❑ BDU0-590-45898-1   *The Glory Field* $4.99

❑ BDU0-590-48668-3   *Slam!* $4.99

❑ BDU0-590-02691-7   *My Name Is America:*
The Journal of Joshua Loper, a Black Cowboy $10.95